IRON MAN 2

0000000000000000
SHSBXCNXMX00000
00202A7A777706E
400A000000000

Little, Brown and Company

Hachette Book Group
237 Park Avenue, New York, NY 10017

Visit our website at www.lb-kids.com

Little, Brown and Company is a division of Hachette Book Group, Inc.
The Little, Brown name and logo are trademarks of Hachette Book Group, Inc.

First edition: April 2010

ISBN 978-0-316-08367-6

10 9 8 7 6 5 4 3 2 1

CWO

Printed in the U.S.A.

IRON MAN 2

MEET THE BLACK WIDOW

Adapted by LISA SHEA

Based on the screenplay by JUSTIN THEROUX

Pictures by GUIDO GUIDI

LB

LITTLE, BROWN AND COMPANY

New York   Boston

When he isn't saving the day
as the Super Hero named Iron Man,
Tony Stark runs a company
called Stark Industries.

Pepper Potts works for Tony.
She used to be his assistant.
Tony was so happy with Pepper,
he gave her a promotion.

Now Tony needs a new assistant.
What about Happy? He is a good friend.
But Happy already has a lot of jobs.
He is Tony's bodyguard and driver.

Happy also works as Tony's trainer
and throws punches in a boxing ring.
Being Iron Man is hard work.
Tony needs to stay in shape.

Natalie Rushman shows up at the gym.
She is new at Stark Industries
and has a contract for Tony to sign.
Natalie watches Tony and Happy box.

Tony stops boxing to meet Natalie.
Tony asks about her work experience
and is impressed with her answers.
"Will you be my new assistant?" he asks.
Natalie says yes!

Tony takes everyone to Monaco
so they can watch a car race.
At a restaurant, Tony and Pepper
try to order water, but the waiter
only speaks French.

Natalie comes to the rescue.
She speaks French very well.
Pepper sees that Natalie
is good at her job.

As Pepper watches Natalie,
she notices some strange things.
When Natalie's phone rings,
she walks away to answer it.

Pepper follows her.

She hears Natalie say,

"Tony Stark just arrived."

Pepper steps forward in anger.

"Who are you talking to?" she asks.

Natalie says it's her dad,

but Pepper does not think that is the truth.

"Your job is to protect Tony,"
Pepper scolds her.
"Do not tell people where he is."

The women walk back to Happy.

Tony has a surprise for everyone:

he is going to drive one of the race cars!

Natalie slips away again. She makes another secret phone call.
"I didn't know. He told no one,"
Natalie whispers. Who is she calling?

Suddenly, a villain named Whiplash stomps onto the racetrack.
Tony has never seen him before.
He's shocked when Whiplash attacks!

Whiplash wears a power source
like the one on the Iron Man suit.
Tony fights his attacker.
Later, the police take Whiplash away.

Tony goes home to rest,
but soon a friend comes to visit.
Nick Fury works for S.H.I.E.L.D.,
a group that tries to keep people safe.

Nick tells Tony to be careful.

Tony has many enemies, such as Whiplash.

"I have someone I want you to meet," Nick says.

"She can help you."

A woman wearing dark clothes
enters the room.
Nick introduces her as Natasha Romanoff.
But she is Tony's assistant, Natalie!
"Natalie is not my real name," she says.

She works undercover for S.H.I.E.L.D.
Just as Tony fights as Iron Man,
she goes by the name Black Widow!
Earlier, Black Widow was making phone
calls to help S.H.I.E.L.D keep Tony safe.

Meanwhile, Whiplash escapes!
He busts through a wall
to get out of jail.

Whiplash sets up a workshop in an abandoned warehouse. There, he builds powerful attack robots. Who is his first target? Iron Man!

A few days later, Whiplash sneaks his robots into a show of new inventions.
Pepper, Happy, and Black Widow are there.

A surprise guest shows up.

He is Iron Man!

He scans the robots' power source

and sees that Whiplash built them!

27

The robots fire at Iron Man!
The hero is strong, but he needs help —
there are just too many enemies.

Where is Whiplash?

He might arrive for a fight, too.

"Find his hideout!" says Iron Man.

Black Widow and Happy go to look.

They soon find Whiplash's workshop.

They break in, but guards try to stop them.

Happy knocks out a guard with one punch.

"Look, I got one!" he yells.

But Black Widow isn't impressed.
She already knocked out twelve guards
and checked the building for Whiplash.
"Whiplash must have left already," she says.
"Let's go help Iron Man."

Black Widow arrives just in time
to help Iron Man fight his enemies.
She's now on Iron Man's team
and ready to save the day!